Will Harry be able to climb the rope?

"Okay, who's next?" the teacher asked.

"Me," Harry said, boldly standing up in the circle.

Everyone stared at Harry.

It was pin-quiet until Song Lee started clapping. "You can do it, Harry!" she said.

Harry saluted Song Lee, then everyone else. We all saluted him back.

"Have a good climb, Harry," Mr. Deltoid said.

Harry unbuttoned the two top buttons of his shirt, then tucked it inside his jeans. When he grabbed the rope, he paused and closed his eyes. I knew what he was doing—saying a silent prayer. I said one too.

OTHER BOOKS IN THE HORRIBLE HARRY SERIES

Horrible Harry and the Ant Invasion
Horrible Harry and the Christmas Surprise
Horrible Harry and the Dead Letters
Horrible Harry and the Dragon War
Horrible Harry and the Drop of Doom
Horrible Harry and the Dungeon
Horrible Harry and The Goog
Horrible Harry and the Green Slime
Horrible Harry and the Holidaze
Horrible Harry and the Kickball Wedding
Horrible Harry and the Locked Closet
Horrible Harry and the Mud Gremlins
Horrible Harry and the Purple People
Horrible Harry and the Triple Revenge
Horrible Harry at Halloween
Horrible Harry Bugs the Three Bears
Horrible Harry Cracks the Code
Horrible Harry Goes to Sea
Horrible Harry Goes to the Moon
Horrible Harry in Room 2B
Horrible Harry Moves Up to Third Grade
Horrible Harry Takes the Cake
Horrible Harry's Secret

HORRIBLE HARRY
on the Ropes

BY **SUZY KLINE**

PICTURES BY **AMY WUMMER**

PUFFIN BOOKS
An Imprint of Penguin Group (USA) Inc.

PUFFIN BOOKS
Published by the Penguin Group
Penguin Young Readers Group, 345 Hudson Street, New York, New York 10014, U.S.A.
Penguin Group (Canada), 90 Eglinton Avenue East, Suite 700,
Toronto, Ontario, Canada M4P 2Y3 (a division of Pearson Penguin Canada Inc.)
Penguin Books Ltd, 80 Strand, London WC2R 0RL, England
Penguin Ireland, 25 St Stephen's Green, Dublin 2, Ireland
(a division of Penguin Books Ltd)
Penguin Group (Australia), 250 Camberwell Road,
Camberwell, Victoria 3124, Australia
(a division of Pearson Australia Group Pty Ltd)
Penguin Books India Pvt Ltd, 11 Community Centre,
Panchsheel Park, New Delhi - 110 017, India
Penguin Group (NZ), 67 Apollo Drive, Rosedale, North Shore 0632, New Zealand
(a division of Pearson New Zealand Ltd)
Penguin Books (South Africa) (Pty) Ltd, 24 Sturdee Avenue,
Rosebank, Johannesburg 2196, South Africa

Registered Offices: Penguin Books Ltd, 80 Strand, London WC2R 0RL, England

First published in the United States of America by Viking,
a division of Penguin Young Readers Group, 2009
Published by Puffin Books, a division of Penguin Young Readers Group, 2011

3 5 7 9 10 8 6 4 2

Illustrations by Amy Wummer

THE LIBRARY OF CONGRESS HAS CATALOGED THE VIKING EDITION AS FOLLOWS:
Kline, Suzy.
Horrible Harry on the ropes / by Suzy Kline ; pictures by Amy Wummer.
p. cm.
Summary: A special Valentine's Day card helps third-grader Harry overcome his fear of climbing the rope in gym class.
ISBN: 978-0-670-01097-4 (hc)
[1. Schools—Fiction. 2. Fear—Fiction. 3. Valentine's Day—Fiction.]
I. Wummer, Amy, ill. II. Title
PZ7.K6797Hpk 2009
[Fic]—dc22 2008044687

Puffin Books ISBN 978-0-14-241695-2

Set in New Century Schoolbook
Printed in the United States of America

For my daughter, Ems.

Thank you for all the love,

laughter, tears, and

stories you bring to my daily life.

You are a blessing to me. I love you!

—Mom

Special thanks to:

Linda Breder, librarian at Riverview School in Denville, New Jersey, and the wonderful pizza lunch group who shared their experiences in gym class climbing a rope:

Kyle Brenner
Adrienne Dell'Aquila
Chrissy Esposito
Conor Fitzgerald
Allyson Handabaka
Serena Lakhiani
Sean Lorenz
Kara Marinelli
Cristina Punzo
Nicholas Schnuriger
Lauren Scornavacca
Nicole Van Hoven
Haley Venezia
Erika C.
Katie G.
Abbey M.

Brad Johnson's article "Rope Climbing Techniques for Fun and Fitness" in *Girevik Magazine*, Issue 2.

Chris Keithan at Birch Grove School, who helped me with the P.E. charts. Thanks for making gym class so much fun for my grandchildren.

My son-in-law, Victor Hurtuk, who is a great physical education teacher.

My grandson, Jake, who talked to me about rope climbing at school.

My granddaughter, Mikenna, who made me a beautiful valentine.

My husband, Rufus, for his sense of humor.

And Catherine Frank, for being such a wonderful editor.

Contents

Valentine's Day Is Coming!

My name is Doug, and I'm in third grade. My friend Harry and I are very excited about Valentine's Day! It's only two days away, and this year, Room 3B has a genuine blue mailbox for all the valentines.

"Don't forget," ZuZu announced, "tomorrow is the last day to mail your valentines. My carriers need time to deliver the heavy mail." It was ZuZu's turn to be postmaster.

Ida and Mary were the new mail carriers.

"Hey, Harry," I said. "Did you finish making all your cards?"

"All but one," Harry said. "Song Lee's." Then he flashed a toothy smile. "I'm still drawing bugs. Want to hear the poem I wrote for her?"

"Sure," I said, looking over his shoulder.

A rose smells sweet.
Lilac smells sweeter.
A stink bug smells like bananas,
But you better not eat her.

"What do you think, Doug?"

I cringed. "Do stink bugs really smell like bananas?"

"Actually," Harry said, "they smell like rotten ones, but I didn't want to put that on a valentine for Song Lee."

"Good idea," I replied. "But what about all those stink bugs? Aren't they going to gross her out?"

"Nah! Song Lee *loves* insects, bugs, and slimy things. Remember? She brought in a potato beetle for show-and-tell in kindergarten. Why do you think I like her?"

"Because she's nice and pretty?"

Before Harry could agree, Sid stopped by his desk. "I picked out the perfect card for you!" he announced. He was holding a valentine in the shape of a yellow bird. "Isn't it great?" he chuckled. "Perfect for Harry the canary!"

"What a coincidence!" Harry said. "I found the perfect one for you too, a squid for Sid."

Sidney popped Harry's valentine inside an envelope and dropped it into the mailbox. "I'm done here!" he said, flipping the lid closed.

"Do you really have a squid valentine?" I whispered.

"No," Harry said. "But I wrote Sid a squid poem."

Just then the teacher called out, "It's one thirty, boys and girls. Time for gym! Which row is ready?"

Harry and I quickly sat up straight and folded our hands.

"Row three may line up."

Harry and I made a beeline for the door.

We were first in line.

Sid was right behind us.

"I can't wait!" he said as we walked down the hall. "Our gym teacher, Mr. Deltoid, is doing a new activity this week, and I know what it is! I saw him setting up this morning when I was taking the lunch count to the cafeteria."

"Don't tell me," Harry said. "I want to be surprised."

When Sid zipped his lips, Harry slapped him five.

We continued our walk down the stairs to the basement just like every Tuesday and Thursday. All the girls were wearing long pants. As we got closer to the gym, we spotted the new posters on the wall.

"Look!" Mary said. "Harry got his name on the 'I Can Do Two Chin-Ups or More' chart."

"And he got his name on the 'I Can Run Ten Gym Laps in Five Minutes' chart like Song Lee, Ida, ZuZu, and me," I added proudly.

Harry, ZuZu, and I held up two fingers.

Song Lee and Ida jumped up and down.

Sidney started dragging his feet. "I almost got on those charts!" he barked.

"You will, too," Song Lee said. "You are very good in gym."

"Do you really think so?" Sid asked.

"Yes, I do," Song Lee replied. "Last week you walked on the balance beam every time without falling."

Sid smiled. He was probably remembering the two times Harry fell off the beam. Song Lee was the best person in Room 3B on the balance beam. She knew what it took to be good in gym.

Sidney's pace suddenly changed. He was walking briskly on his toes now.

As soon as we got to the door and

could see into the gym, Harry made an abrupt stop.

Sid crashed right into him.

"Whoa!" he said into Harry's back.

Harry didn't move. He just kept staring into the gym.

Miss Mackle turned around. "Come along, children, Mr. Deltoid is waiting."

As soon as I saw it, I knew what was freaking Harry out.

Mr. Deltoid's Gym Class

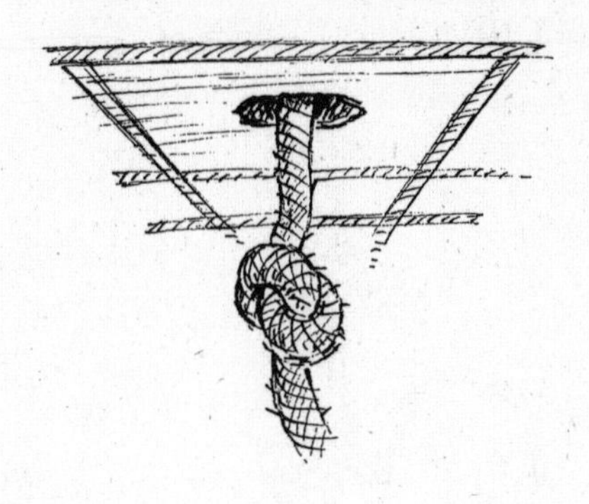

The climbing rope!

It hung from a hole in the ceiling. It was thick and had ten equally spaced knots. Each one was about the size of my two fists.

Quickly, we sat in a circle that surrounded the rope. Mr. Deltoid stood in the middle on a large blue mat and welcomed us. "Are you ready for a new exciting activity this week?"

Everyone shouted *"Yeah!"* except Harry.

"Looks like fun," Miss Mackle said on her way out of the gym.

"It *is* fun!" Mr. Deltoid said. "I'll show you, kids."

We all watched our gym teacher grab the rope. "First, you want to put the rope between your thighs and curl your feet around the end. One foot will be in front, and the other will be behind the rope."

So far, so good, I thought.

"Then you reach up and place your hands on the rope like this—always one directly on top of the other."

We watched our gym teacher inch his way up the rope as he talked. "Pull your body up with your arms.

When your chest reaches the level of your hands, squeeze the rope with your legs and feet. Now you can reach up higher with one hand, then the other."

Harry couldn't look anymore. He started retying his sneakers. I knew he was afraid of heights. Last year when Song Lee had her end-of-the-year party at an amusement park, Harry had the same problem with going on the Drop of Doom ride.

Mr. Deltoid zipped up the rope to the second, third, and fourth knots. "This activity really develops strength in your forearms. You'll also feel the muscles working in your shoulders and elbows."

Some of us started flexing our arms.

Sidney acted like he was lifting dumb-bells.

"Look!" ZuZu said. "Mr. Deltoid is almost at the top of the rope!"

Harry covered his eyes with both hands.

Everyone else cheered and clapped for our gym teacher as he made it to the ceiling.

"What can you see up there?" ZuZu called out.

Mr. Deltoid hung on to the top of the rope as he looked at the back wall. "Well," he said, "I can see out the small window here at the top of the gym."

"Cool," Sidney said. "What do you see?"

"A car that needs a hubcap."

Some of us laughed.

"What else do you see?" Mary asked.

"Well, actually, there's a hole at the top of this rope that goes into the ceiling. It's big enough to put your hand inside."

Harry immediately looked up. I knew he would be curious about that hole. Harry loves being a detective. "Can you see anything in there?" he blurted out.

Mr. Deltoid took one hand off the rope and reached into the hole. "There is something roundish in here. Oh! It's just an old gum wad."

"Eweyee!" lots of kids said.

"That's gross!" Mary complained.

"Cool!" Harry said. He likes horrible things. "What color is it?" he asked.

"Gray, with a few hairs," Mr. Deltoid called out.

"Eweyee!" Now everyone groaned—except Harry, of course.

Mr. Deltoid quickly moved down the rope, then jumped onto the blue mat. He took a small bottle of hand sanitizer out of his back pocket and wiped his hands. "So who wants to go first?"

Room 3B on the Ropes

ROPE CLIMBERS			
Sidney			

Mr. Deltoid looked at our class.

Only a half dozen kids raised their hands. Sidney waved his back and forth, calling out, "I do! I do! I do!"

"Okay, Sid. You can go first. I like your enthusiasm."

"I'm good at climbing. I have a tree-house with a rope at home, so I'm used to it."

"That's great, Sid! Practice is everything," Mr. Deltoid replied.

I was planning to go up too, but not right away. I wanted to watch other kids do it first.

Sid started out just like the teacher did. He reached up and grabbed the rope with both hands, curling his feet around the end. "You're looking at Spider-Man!" he joked.

As I looked over at Harry, I noticed he was able to watch now.

Inch by inch, Sid hoisted himself up, putting one hand directly on top of the other. When he got to the fifth knot, which was halfway up, he shouted, "This is *eeeeasy*!" Then he reached up high again and pulled his body upward with his hands, always keeping his feet curled around the rope. When he got to the eighth knot, he looked down at us. "I can see the top of Mr. Deltoid's head!" he exclaimed. "It's shiny!"

Most of us tried not to giggle. Mr. Deltoid had a bald spot there. Usually we didn't see it unless he bent over. When the teacher broke out laughing, we laughed too.

Moments later, our laughing burst into cheers. Sidney had made it to the top!

Sidney La Fleur! What a surprise!

Song Lee and the girls were jumping up and down.

Harry half smiled. "Squids have suckers on their legs. Sid is one good climbing dude!"

Sidney hustled down the rope. As soon as he landed on the blue mat, Mr. Deltoid slapped him ten. "Way to go, Sidney. Fantastic job!"

We could see the palms of Sid's hands. They were red. He rubbed them on his pants.

"So, who's next?" the gym teacher asked.

A dozen people put their hands up.

"If Sidney can do it," Mary said, "I can!"

"Okay, Mary, give it a good try. Just remember: boys have more upper-body strength at this age, so don't get discouraged."

"Not me," Mary bragged. "You're looking at Spider-*Woman*!"

The girls cheered her on.

Mary got to the second knot and stopped.

"Good try!" Mr. Deltoid said. "Now, come on down, Mary."

"I can't move!" she said. "I can't go up or down. I'm stuck!" she exclaimed.

Mr. Deltoid moved right next to her. "I'll catch you if you want to drop down. You're not up high."

"You won't drop me, will you?" Mary whimpered.

"I will not drop you, Mary. I'm Mr. Muscle Man!"

Some of us chuckled. Mr. Deltoid had a good sense of humor.

Mary slowly let go and dropped from the rope. Mr. Deltoid lowered her down to the mat.

"I'm embarrassed," she said.

"You shouldn't be," the teacher replied. "You tried and that's all that counts. I'm proud of you, Mary!"

Mary slowly nodded, then walked

over to Sidney. "You're amazing! I didn't realize how hard rope climbing was."

Sidney smiled ear to ear. "Thank you, Mary."

Harry immediately went up to the teacher and whispered something in his ear. After Mr. Deltoid gave an answer, Harry let out a deep breath.

"You don't have to try the rope today if you don't want to," the teacher said. "You can watch and learn from the other kids."

As it turned out, Sidney was the only one in Room 3B to make it to the top. I made it to the fourth knot, and Song Lee made it halfway, but most kids didn't get past the third knot.

"Can you feel the muscles in your

shoulders, elbows, and forearms?" Mr. Deltoid asked.

"I sure can," I groaned.

"Me too. They're sore," ZuZu admitted.

"No pain, no gain—that's what some people say." Mr. Deltoid chuckled. "But I want you guys to stop when you're feeling any discomfort. Okay?"

We all nodded.

"You did a super job today, and Sidney, I'm putting your name on a new chart for rope climbing. Making it to the top is quite an achievement for a third grader."

Song Lee was the first one to start clapping.

Sidney jumped up and down. "Yahoo!" he shouted. "I'm on the climbing chart!"

Miss Mackle clapped from the doorway. "Way to go, Sidney La Fleur! And class, I am so proud of *all* of you for trying."

"But we didn't *all* try!" Mary complained.

Harry immediately looked down at the blue mat. He didn't want anyone to see his eyes. They were getting a little watery.

"Harry just wanted to watch today," Mr. Deltoid explained. "And I told him that was just fine. I'll bet he tries on Thursday."

"I'll bet he does too," Miss Mackle agreed.

Harry kept staring down at the floor.

When we walked over to the door, Harry lined up last. I joined him at the end of the line. So did Song Lee.

“Are you okay?” Song Lee whispered.

“Yeah . . . sure,” Harry mumbled, but he didn’t look up.

Song Lee and I exchanged a look. We knew Harry was dreading Thursday. He was going to need lots of help to get on that rope.

Song Lee's Special Valentine

On Wednesday afternoon during activity time, everyone in Room 3B was doing different things. Some kids were on the computers, some were sharing a book in the library corner, a few were writing stories together, and some of us were drawing.

"Does everyone have their valentines mailed?" ZuZu asked.

"I do!" Sid blurted out.

"I do!" most people responded.

"I'm almost ready," Song Lee said softly.

Sidney left his computer and walked over to her desk. "What valentine have you been working on so long?" he asked politely.

I looked up from my drawing.

Song Lee seemed too embarrassed to say anything.

"It says, 'For Someone Special!'" Sidney read out loud. "How cool is that? Your card even has red felt hearts and red velvet ribbon on the front." Sid opened it up and saw a small box of candy hearts inside. "Wow!" he exclaimed. His eye caught mine, and I nodded. It was cool!

Then Sid left her desk and stopped

by mine. "We know who the special person is *this week,* right Doug?" he whispered.

"Your name's going on the 'Climbing Rope' chart!" I said slapping him five. *Oh boy*, I thought, as Sid skipped over to his computer. He was sure that valentine was for him!

I was glad to go back to my project. I was using a ruler to make a tall building. Harry was concentrating hard on his drawing. It was a picture of our climbing rope in gym class. It had ten hairy knots.

"I figured it out, Doug," he said.

"What?" I answered. I was busy making bricks.

"I figured out how many times you

have to hoist yourself up the rope."

"You're still thinking about that?" I asked.

"I have to. I'm no scaredy-cat."

"Of course you're no scaredy-cat, Harry!"

"Well, I looked like one yesterday."

"So, do you have a plan?" Harry usually had a plan for things.

"Yes, I do. I think I can make it halfway tomorrow, which is a good enough

try, if I just count slowly to twenty-five, don't look down, and don't think about falling or smashing my bones to bits."

I cringed and shivered.

"What's with the number twenty-five?" I said, hoping to change the subject from smashed bones.

"When Sid went up, it took him about five hand pulls between knots. I counted them."

"Sounds good, Harry," I said. "Count as you climb."

At that moment, Song Lee walked over to the mailbox with her special valentine. It was addressed with a red pen and a rose sticker. Sidney rushed over, but just as he did, she dropped it into the slot and flipped the lid.

Sidney didn't seem disappointed not to see the name on the envelope. He was singing, "Hip-hip hurray for Valentine's Day! I can't wait for tomorrow!"

Valentine's Day!

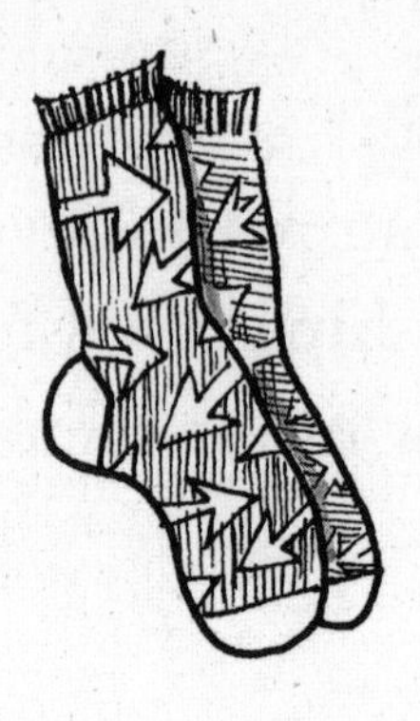

On Thursday morning, even though it was a regular gym day, most kids dressed up in red and pink. All the girls wore pants as usual, but some had bows and ribbons in their hair. Ida wore a heart necklace. Mary was wearing a pink sweatshirt with red hearts on it. Song Lee had a red-and-black ladybug barrette in her hair.

Sidney was wearing jeans with a shirt and red tie. Harry brushed his hair for the first time since Picture Day. I thought the red socks my grandma gave me were cool. They had white arrows on them.

After we had reading and writing and math, it was noon.

Most of us were eating hot lunch, because it was "Finger Food Day" in our cafeteria. You don't have to use silverware. I like dipping the chicken fingers in honey, the carrot sticks in ranch dressing, and the French fries in ketchup. Our school cook, Mrs. Funderburke, was stopping by each table wishing kids a happy Valentine's Day. When she came to Room 3B's table, she made a beeline for Sidney. "You sure look handsome in that tie," she said.

"It's a special day for a special guy," Sidney chuckled. Then he glanced over at Song Lee. She was eating from a container of kimchi, a special Korean vegetable dish. Her mom packed it often for her lunch.

"Well, don't break too many hearts, Sidney," Mrs. Funderburke teased.

Sidney chuckled with delight. "Miss Mackle loved my tie too. I can't wait until Mr. Deltoid sees it in gym today."

"Maybe you'll inspire him to wear one some day!" Mrs. Funderburke joked.

Harry tugged on her apron to get her attention. His mouth was still full of chicken. "You're the best cook in the world!" he said.

Mrs. Funderburke giggled. "You're my biggest fan, Harry!" And then she patted his head. "Nice hairdo!"

Harry beamed.

As soon as our cook left, Harry lowered his voice. "I think I can do this, Doug. I think I can make it halfway up the rope. Just count and climb." Then Harry waved the chicken finger like a baton and started counting, "One . . . two . . . three."

I kept time with him by popping goldfish crackers into my mouth, "four . . . five . . . six. . . ."

At one o'clock, when we returned to class after lunch recess, all the valentines were on our desks.

"Good job delivering the mail!" ZuZu called out.

Ida and Mary beamed. "We had to

stay in during lunch recess. There were so many to deliver!"

Miss Mackle went to the front of the room. "Enjoy reading your valentines, class. At one thirty we'll go to gym, then come back for our party."

Lots of us cheered as we began ripping open our valentines.

"I like your Elvis Presley valentine, Dexter!" Mary said.

"It's an authentic Elvis too," Dexter replied. "He's got blue suede shoes."

I read Harry's valentine out loud. He wrote a riddle for me.

"'What fast animal sits on your head?' I give up, Harry. What is it?"

"A hare." Harry giggled. "Get it, Doug-o? Like a hair on your head?"

I cracked up. I was glad to see Harry feeling better about things.

"Hey, Harry," Sidney said, "I like your squid poem. Who wants to hear it?"

A few of us nearby said yes.

"Squids have eight legs,
suckers, and goo.
You can be one for Halloween,
and say, boo, boo, boo, boo,
boo, boo, boo, boo!"

"Get it?" Harry added. "Eight boos for eight legs."

"*Booooooooo!*" Mary groaned. "And that's one big boo! Don't you know what holiday we're celebrating? It's Valentine's Day, not Halloween."

Harry just grinned like a jack-o'-lantern. He loves writing horrible poems.

It didn't bother Sidney, either. He

kept humming as he went through his valentines. When he got to the last one, he straightened his red tie.

"I'm saving the best for last," Sidney declared. "And I know who sent it, Song Lee! There's a bulge in it for a small box of candy hearts."

I watched Sidney open the white envelope.

He stopped humming and smiling as he looked inside. "Hey," he groaned. "It doesn't say, 'For Someone Special.'"

The card said *Happy Valentine's Day! From your friend, Song Lee.* Inside was a small box of candy hearts.

Sidney opened the box and dumped the contents in his hand. One by one he popped them into his mouth. After he finished, he picked up the empty box and squished it.

By the time he stomped over to Harry's desk, Sid was seething.

Harry had three more valentines to open. Sidney picked up the one on his desk that had a bulge in it. "Open this one next," he snapped.

Harry did. It was Song Lee's beautiful valentine *For Someone Special.*

Harry's eyebrows went up like an elevator. "Neat-o!" he said, rubbing his fingers along the red velvet ribbon. He put the box of candy in his jeans pocket, set the card down, and then made a beeline for Song Lee's desk.

"Thank you for my valentine," Harry said. "It's the best one I've ever gotten."

Song Lee glowed. "I like your poem too," she said. "And your eight colorful stink bugs."

Harry flashed a toothy smile. Song Lee had counted them. "I made eight bugs because you're eight years old."

"That's so nice, Harry," she replied.

I looked up at the clock while they

stared at each other. It was one thirty!

"Which row is ready to line up?" Miss Mackle said.

Harry was in a daze, still staring at Song Lee.

"Harry," I called. "It's time for *gym!*"

"Gym" was the magic word that got Harry's attention. He rushed back to his seat. As soon as he got there, he didn't sit down and fold his hands. He was looking around for something.

"Row two may line up," the teacher said. "Row four. Row one."

A full minute later, Harry finally sat down.

"Okay, row three may line up."

"Man," I complained, "we're last in

line, Harry. What were you looking for?"

Harry gritted his teeth. "That special valentine Song Lee gave me. It's *gone!*"

"Gone?" I gasped. "Where could it be?"

The Zipped Sweater Jacket

As we hurried down the hall, Harry and I talked about his missing valentine.

"It wasn't there when I got back to my desk," Harry explained. "I left it right on top too. It had that red velvet bow on the front. You can't miss it."

"Did you check the floor under your desk?"

"Yes, and my chair, and I even looked inside my desk."

"The inside of your desk?" I asked. "That's another universe!"

Harry didn't laugh. He pointed to Sidney. He was a few steps ahead of us in line.

"Hey, why is he wearing that zipped-up sweater jacket? Gym is indoors today."

"He doesn't want Mr. Deltoid to see his tie?" I guessed.

"But he does. Remember what Sid said at noontime?"

"Oh, yeah," I recalled. "He couldn't wait for Mr. Deltoid to see it."

"So why is he hiding his tie?"

"Oh, man," I said. "Do you think . . . ?"

"Yup," Harry snapped. "He's hiding something *else* inside that jacket." Slowly, Harry raised a fist.

Uh oh, I thought. Sid was doomed! As soon as we got inside the gym, Harry hurried over to Sidney. He put his nose right next to his. "Okay buster, fork it over!" he said.

Sid took a step back. "Fork what over?"

"You know what," Harry snarled. "And I know *where* you have it too. My valentine is hidden in your sweater."

"You're crazy, Harry," Sid replied.

"Yeah? Well, then prove me wrong. Unzip it!"

Just then a booming voice called out, "Find your spot in the circle, please, and sit down."

"I'll . . . d-do it r-right . . . after class," Sidney stammered. "I promise."

Harry glared at Sidney as he hurried over to his spot. The mats were all set up, and the climbing rope was still in the middle, hanging down from the ceiling.

"Happy Valentine's Day, kids!"

"Happy Valentine's Day, Mr. Deltoid!" we all answered.

"Thank you. Now, are we ready to climb the rope this afternoon?"

"Yes!"

"Okay, who wants to go first?"

Sidney stood tall. "Me!"

"All right!" Mr. Deltoid said.

Sidney jumped up like he was riding a pogo stick.

"You don't have to go all the way to the top this time, Sid," Mr. Deltoid said. "Be sure to stop when it doesn't feel comfortable. Okay?"

"Okay," Sid answered. He rubbed his hands together and then grabbed the rope. He pulled it close to his chest, reaching up high with his hands and curling his legs around the bottom.

Everyone watched Sidney inch his way upward. He went faster this time, and didn't stop to make a comment.

"He's unbelievable on that rope!" Mary said.

"Go, Sidney!" Song Lee and Ida chanted.

Sidney kept putting one hand in front of the other, pulling himself up higher and higher. When he got to the top, everyone applauded. And that's when he dropped a coin.

"Ooops! Sorry, I dropped a penny. Look out below!" he called.

Everyone looked down at the floor to see where it landed.

And then a few seconds later, Sid made his descent and let go of the rope.

"Well done, Sid!" Mr. Deltoid cheered. "Let's give him a hand."

And we did.

"Okay, Ida, you can go next," the teacher said.

While Ida began her climb up the rope, Harry went over to Sidney's spot. It looked like he was congratulating him, but I knew better. He wanted Sid to unzip that jacket.

I couldn't hear them, but I could see their faces. Sid didn't look nervous anymore. He unzipped his sweater right away. No valentine fell out of it. When Harry returned, his eyebrows were lowered. I knew he was thinking hard.

"It wasn't there?" I asked.

"Nope," Harry said, gritting his teeth. "Sid hid it somewhere. Somewhere in this gym . . ."

"That valentine would be hard to hide," I said. "It has a bright red bow. I don't see it anywhere. Do you think

he stashed it under one of the blue mats?"

"No, because someone would have seen him do it. There are twenty witnesses in this gym."

"Look at Ida go!" Mary yelled. She and Song Lee started clapping.

Harry and I looked up.

"She passed the third knot," I said. "She's doing great, huh?"

Harry didn't say a word. His eyes were glued to the top of the rope.

"Holey moley!" he exclaimed. "Take a look at that hole in the ceiling, Doug."

I put my head back and looked up. "There's something . . . red sticking out!"

"Bingo!" Harry replied. "It's the red velvet ribbon on my valentine. Sid stashed it up there while everyone was looking for his dropped penny. Clever guy, huh?"

"He sure is," I agreed. "It's the perfect hiding place. Sid knows he's the *only* one who can climb to the top."

"Well, he's wrong about that."

"What do you mean, Harry? You're not going up that rope?"

"I sure am."

"No, way! Just tell the teacher, Harry. Mr. Deltoid will get your valentine and Sidney will get in big trouble."

"Nope. I have to do it myself. Besides, I'm no tattletale. It's my valentine and I'm getting it."

"All right," I said. "But you'd better say a prayer first before you start climbing."

Harry on the Climbing Rope

Ida jumped down to the blue mat.

"What a good climb, Ida!" Mr. Deltoid said. "You made it to the fifth knot! That's two more than last time. Let's give her a hand, everyone."

We all clapped and cheered for Ida.

"Okay, who's next?" the teacher asked.

"Me," Harry said, boldly standing up in the circle.

Everyone stared at Harry.

It was pin-quiet until Song Lee started clapping. "You can do it, Harry!" she said.

Harry saluted Song Lee, then everyone else. We all saluted him back.

"Have a good climb, Harry," Mr. Deltoid said.

Harry unbuttoned the two top buttons of his shirt, then tucked it inside his jeans. When he grabbed the rope, he paused and closed his eyes. I knew what he was doing—saying a silent prayer. I said one too.

Suddenly, he began inching his way up.

"Go, Harry!" the guys called out.

Harry never looked back on his climb

upward. He kept his eyes on the next knot. I wondered if he was counting. When he got to the second knot, I could see his hands trembling, but he kept going. When he got to the fifth knot, he didn't stop, he just kept going.

"You're doing great, Harry!" Song Lee shouted. Then she covered her mouth. She had never been that loud before in class.

Other kids were cheering him on too. "Be sure to stop when you want to, Harry," Mr. Deltoid cautioned. He was holding the bottom of the rope steady. "You don't have to go all the way up."

"He has to stop soon," Sidney said confidently. "He doesn't like heights."

Harry didn't respond to any of us; he just kept inching his way up. His feet were curled around the rope very tightly. Every time they reached a new knot, he took a deep breath and continued upward.

When he got to the eighth knot, and then the ninth, Sidney's eyes started to bug out.

I closed mine—I was so nervous for Harry, I couldn't watch anymore. *Hang on to that rope!* I thought. *Hang on to that rope!*

Suddenly Mary blurted out, "Harry made it!"

When I opened my eyes, everyone was clapping and cheering. Harry was at the top of the rope right next to the hole.

I started jumping up and down. "Way to go, Harry!" And then I added, "Don't let go!"

"Bravo!" Mr. Deltoid said. "Take a moment now, Harry, catch your breath before you come down."

Harry put one hand in the hole while holding very tightly to the rope with the other.

"Look out for the hairy gum wad!" ZuZu warned.

Harry didn't say a word.

He didn't look down.

I knew when he was moving his elbows around, he was stuffing that valentine in his shirt. Everyone else was looking at each other and chuckling about the gum.

Everyone . . . except Sidney. His mouth was wide open.

I knew what he was thinking, *Did Harry get it*?

At that moment, Harry started making his descent. He didn't go fast. He took it slow and easy.

Finally, when Harry reached the second knot, he slid down the rest of the way and jumped onto the blue mat. His whole body was shaking.

Everyone was clapping and cheering for Harry.

"You did it!" Mr. Deltoid said. "Awesome job!"

"*Yeah* for Harry!" Song Lee called out, jumping in the air like a cheerleader.

"Can you tell us the weather outside the top window?" ZuZu asked.

Harry was a little out of breath but he managed an answer. "It was . . . snow . . . ing . . . a . . . lit . . . tle."

Now, everyone cheered again.

"I'm adding Harry's name to my Climbing Rope chart," Mr. Deltoid said proudly.

Song Lee went over to Harry and hugged him. He hugged her back.

"I did it!" Harry said.

When he came over to me, I could see the beads of sweat on the side of his face. And his hair was a little wet too. "Show me . . . some . . . knuck . . . les, Doug!" Harry said, still a little out of breath.

And that's when we did our double-knuckle five.

"Did the counting help?" I whispered.

"The praying did," Harry whispered back.

"You're one cool dude!" I replied.

"Thanks," Harry said. Then he added,

"Excuse me, Doug-o, I have to go to the bathroom."

When Harry returned a few minutes later, Dexter was on the rope. Harry and I walked over to Sid's spot in the circle and sat next to him. I didn't want to miss a word of the conversation this time.

"Hey, Sid," Harry began. "That hole is pretty interesting."

"Yeah. Did . . . did you s-see the g-gum?" Sid stammered.

"Yes, I did. And something else. Guess what it was, Sid?"

Sidney's eyes started to bug out again. "I d-don't . . . kn-know," he mumbled.

"A valentine like *this*, maybe?" Harry pulled Song Lee's card out of his shirt.

"You got it?" Sidney said.

"I sure did."

Sidney started to freak out. "I'm sorry, Harry. I'm really sorry. I promise I'll never steal another valentine from you as long as I live. Cross my heart and hope to die. Stick a fork in my eye."

"Fork? It's a needle, dude," Harry said, staring into the whites of Sidney's eyes.

"I mean 'needle'! I'm nervous about getting in trouble. Are you going to tell the teacher?" Sidney looked desperate.

"I have to think about it," Harry teased.

Now Sidney started to sweat. I could see perspiration rolling down the sides of his cheeks.

"*Please* don't tell," Sidney begged. He got down on his knees. "Pleeeeease."

Harry stared at Sid. "So, why did you take it?"

"Because . . . because I thought I deserved it. I was the only one who could climb that rope. The valentine should have been mine." Just as Sid was about to cry, Harry took the box of candy hearts out of his back pocket. "Okay. I won't tell the teacher."

"You won't?" Sidney immediately stood up.

"Nope." Then Harry added, "Actually, Sid, I need to say thank you."

"Huh? What did you say, Harry?"

"I want to say thank you. And you can have my box of candy hearts that Song Lee gave me, for a reward."

"A reward? For what?" Sid was baffled.

I was too. What was Harry doing?

"It's my way of saying thank you, ol' Sid."

"For taking your special valentine?" Sid looked confused.

"No," Harry replied. "For *hiding it* in

that hole in the ceiling. There's no way I would have ever climbed that rope if it hadn't been for you."

"O . . . kay. So . . . you're not going to tell on me?" Sidney asked again.

"I'm not. You got me up that rope, Sid the squid. Slap me five!"

Sidney slapped Harry five.

I couldn't believe it. I followed Harry as he walked back to our place in the circle. "No big revenge for Sid?" I whispered.

"No big revenge for Sid." Harry giggled. "Just a little Harry one."

Epilogue

Ten minutes later, everyone was settled into Room 3B, munching on heart-shaped cookies and drinking pink lemonade. Miss Mackle was admiring the heart pillow Song Lee's mom had embroidered with all our names written in cursive. Mary's was the neatest. Harry's was the sloppiest.

"Thank you, boys and girls, for your

beautiful Valentine's Day gift. I'll treasure it always."

Suddenly, Sidney let out a terrible shriek.

Everyone stared at Sidney. He was standing up, holding the box of candy Harry had given him in the gym. *"Eweyee!"* Sid squealed. "There's something stuck to three of my candy hearts . . . a wad of gum with hairs on it!"

"Eweyee!" everyone moaned.

"Gross!" Mary added.

I looked at Harry. He was grinning.

"You did that at the top of the rope?" I whispered

"Are you kidding?" Harry lowered his voice. "I did it in the boys' bathroom."

Ah, I thought, *a little sweet hairy revenge.*

ZuZu
Dexter
Song Lee
Mary
We
Miss Mackle
Ida
Sidney
Douglas
Harry